Andrew Curtis White

Memorials of Roderick White and his Wife, Lucy Blakeslee of Paris Hill, N.Y.

with some account of their American ancestors and a complete record of

their descendants

Andrew Curtis White

Memorials of Roderick White and his Wife, Lucy Blakeslee of Paris Hill, N.Y.
with some account of their American ancestors and a complete record of their descendants

ISBN/EAN: 9783337339890

Printed in Europe, USA, Canada, Australia, Japan

Cover: Foto ©Andreas Hilbeck / pixelio.de

More available books at **www.hansebooks.com**

1632-1892.

MEMORIALS

OF

RODERICK WHITE

AND HIS WIFE

LUCY BLAKESLEE

OF

PARIS HILL, N. Y.,

WITH SOME ACCOUNT OF THEIR AMERICAN ANCESTORS AND A
COMPLETE RECORD OF THEIR DESCENDANTS.

BY

ANDREW C. WHITE.

———

Patriis virtutibus.

———

ITHACA, N. Y.
PRINTED FOR THE FAMILY
BY ANDRUS & CHURCH.
1892.

PREFACE.

KELLOGG'S "MEMORIALS OF ELDER JOHN WHITE AND OF HIS DESCENDANTS" is now out of print and difficult to obtain at any price. Since 1860 another generation has sprung up; of the one hundred and twenty-two descendants of Roderick White only twenty-seven are mentioned in that work. At the request of several members of the family, I have prepared this supplement to Kellogg's "Memorials," which is intended to give a continuous record of our branch of the family from the emigration of John White and Thomas Blakeslee to New England down to the present time. In its preparation I have had occasion to consult many printed books, of which I mention the most important. (1) Drake's "Founders of New England," Boston, 1860. It gives the "licenses to pass beyond the seas" of emigrants to New England from 1632 to 1637, as found in the British Public Records. This establishes the date of John White's emigration as June 22, 1632, and that of Thomas Blakeslee's as July 28, 1635. (2) Savage's "Genealogical Dictionary of the First Settlers of New England," Boston, 1860–62,—a work indispensable to every worker in the field of American genealogy. (3) Walker's "Thomas Hooker," N. Y., 1891, which, though mentioning John White by name only as a witness of Hooker's will, gives an admirable picture of the spiritual and physical environment of the Puritan settlers of Connecticut. (4) Bronson's "History of Waterbury," Waterbury, 1858, which contains genealogical notices of the Blakeslee family. Personal information has been sought from many sources, and has been given with unfailing promptness and accuracy. For special aid I wish to thank Professor Aaron White and Mrs. Phebe W. Maltby, of Cazenovia, and the Rev. Marvin P. Blakeslee, of Ithaca.

For convenience of reference Roderick White is distinguished by the number (1) and to his descendants are assigned consecutively in the order of seniority of descent the numbers from (2) to (123). In lists of children the sign + following a number indicates that a further account of the individual and his family is to be found in a subsequent paragraph. A separate paragraph is given to every descendant of Roderick White named White who has had children. A superior figure in lists of direct ancestors marks the number of the generation, counting John White's as the first. Ordinary abbreviations are used freely. Alternate pages have been left blank for the purpose of keeping up the family record in future years. I shall be pleased to receive and to communicate such items of family history as may properly find place in such records.

Of the 122 descendants of Roderick White named in these pages, 14 died in infancy, 3 in early childhood, and 2 about the age of sixty. Of the 103 now living, 52 are residents of New York State, 18 of Kansas, 7 of Michigan, 4 of Connecticut, 4 of Ohio, 1 of Illinois, and 17 of Canada. It is my hope that the Memorials here presented may help to keep united in interest and sympathy our family now so widely scattered.

ANDREW C. WHITE.

Ithaca, Sept. 9, 1892.

American Ancestry of Roderick White.

FIRST GENERATION.

ELDER JOHN WHITE, who was born in England, about 1600, arrived at Boston by the ship Lyon from London, September 16, 1632. He was admitted a freeman of Massachusetts, March 4, 1633. In February, 1635, he was chosen one of the first board of selectmen of Cambridge. In 1636 he joined the company of the Rev..Thomas Hooker in founding Hartford on the Connecticut River. In 1659 he was one of the leaders in the settlement of Hadley, in Massachusetts. This town chose him its Deputy to the General Court or Legislature, sitting in Boston, in 1664 and again in 1669. About 1670 he returned to Hartford, and was chosen Ruling Elder in the South Church. In the winter of 1683–84 he rested from his labors. He was a friend and strong supporter of Thomas Hooker, and was one of the witnesses to his will, July 7, 1647. His successive removals from England to Massachusetts, to the wilderness of the Connecticut, to the frontier settlement of Hadley, and again to Hartford, were all prompted by his desire to realize the Puritan ideal of a Church formed after the scriptural model. John White's wife, whom he married in England, had the Christian name of Mary, and died before her husband.

CHILDREN.

1. *Mary*, b. in Eng., about 1625 ; m. Jonathan Gilbert ; d. 1650.
2. *Nathaniel*. b. in Eng., 1629 ; m. 1st, Elizabeth —— ; 2nd, Mrs. Martha Mould ; d. Aug. 27, 1711.
3. *John*, b. about 1632 ; m. Sarah Bunce ; d. Sept., 1665.
4. *Daniel*, b. about 1638 ; m. Sarah Crowe ; d. July 27, 1713.
5. *Sarah*, b. about 1641 ; m. 1st, Stephen Taylor ; 2nd, Barnabas Hinsdale ; 3d, Walter Hickson.
6. *Jacob*, b. Oct. 8, 1645 ; m. Elizabeth Bunce ; d. 1701.

SECOND GENERATION.

Captain NATHANIEL WHITE, (John[1]), eldest son of Elder John White, was born in England, about 1629, three years before

5

the family came to New England.   When about twenty-one years old he removed to Middletown, being one of the original proprietors and first settlers of that town.   He was elected a Representative from Middletown to the General Court eighty-five times, being eighty-one years old when last chosen.   He died Aug. 27, 1711, aged about eighty-two.   He married 1st, Elizabeth ——, who was the mother of his eight children.   She died in 1690, aged about sixty-five.   He married 2nd, Mrs. Martha Mould, widow of Hugh Mould of New London, and dau. of John Coit.   She died April 14, 1730, aged about eighty-six.

CHILDREN.

1. *Nathaniel*, b. July 7, 1652 ; m. Elizabeth Savage ; d. Feb. 15, 1742.
2. *Elizabeth*, b. Mar. 7, 1655 ; m. John Clark ; d. Dec. 25, 1711.
3. *John*, b. April 9, 1657 ; m. Mary —— ; d. July, 1748.
4. *Mary*, b. April 7, 1659 ; m. 1st, Jacob Cornwell ; 2nd, John Bacon ; d. Nov. 15, 1732.
5. *Daniel*, b. Feb. 23, 1661 ; m. Susannah Mould ; d. Dec. 18, 1739.
6. *Sarah*, b. Jan. 22, 1664 ; m. John Smith ; d. before her father.
7. *Jacob*, b. May 10, 1665 ; m. 1st, Deborah Shepard ; 2nd, Rebecca Ranney ; d. Mar. 29, 1738.
8. *Joseph*, b. Feb. 20, 1667 ; m. Mary Mould ; d. Feb. 28, 1725.

THIRD GENERATION.

Ensign DANIEL WHITE. (Nathaniel[2], John[1]), third son of Capt. Nathaniel White, was born at Middletown, Upper Houses, Feb. 23, 1661.*   He lived in his native place, and was chosen a townsman, or selectman, of Middletown in 1690, and a constable in 1701.   He died Dec. 18, 1739, aged seventy-eight.   He married, March, 1683, Susannah Mould, dau. of Hugh Coit, of New London, by whom he had eleven children.   Her mother, Martha Coit, became the second wife of Capt. Nathaniel White.   Mrs. Susannah White was born April 2, 1663, and died Sept. 7, 1754.

CHILDREN.

1. *Daniel*, b. Dec. 8, 1683 ; m. Alice Cook ; d. Jan. 10, 1758.
2. *Nathaniel*, b. Sept. 3, 1685 ; m. Mehitable Hurlburt ; d. May 5, 1743.
3. *Joseph*, b. —— ; d. Oct. 8, 1687.
4. *Joseph*, b. Oct. 8, 1688 ; m. 1st, Mary Hall ; 2nd, Abigail Butler ; 3d, Mrs. Lois Bliss ; d. Dec. 14, 1770.
5. *Hugh*, b. Feb. 15, 1691 ; m. Mary Stone ; d. Mar. 1, 1778.   His young-

---

* So the town record.   See Appendix II.

est son, Hugh White, b. Jan. 25, 1733, was the Pioneer in the settlement of Central New York, giving name to Whitestown; d. April 16, 1812.

6. *John*, b. Nov. 27, 1692; m. Susannah Alling; d. Jan. 15, 1783.

7. *Susannah*, b. Oct. 16, 1694; m. Thomas Johnson; d. Sept. 28, 1786.

8. *Isaac*, b. Nov. 9, 1696; m. Sibbil Butler; d. June 26, 1768.

9. *Jonathan*, bap. Mar. 30, 1701; d. May 7, 1702.

10. *Ruth*, b. Sept. 28, 1703; m. Jehiel Stone; d. Mar. 28, 1774.

11. *Rachel*, b. Feb. 3, 1705; m. William Chittenden, jun.; d. Oct. 15, 1752.

FOURTH GENERATION.

Deacon ISAAC WHITE (Daniel[3], Nathaniel[2], John[1]), seventh and youngest surviving son of Ensign Daniel White, was born at Middletown, Upper Houses, Nov. 9, 1696, and settled there. He was constable in 1735 and selectman from 1746 to 1749. He was chosen a deacon of the church there, Jan. 15, 1749. He died June 26, 1768*, aged seventy-one. He married, June 30, 1726, Sibbil Butler, dau. of Thomas Butler of Hartford. She was born March 6, 1702, and died Nov. 7, 1781, aged seventy-nine.

CHILDREN.

1. *Moses*, b. Aug. 22, 1727; m. Huldah Knowles; d. Oct. 12, 1796.

2. *Martha*, b. Oct. 27, 1728; d. unm. April 1, 1813.

3. *Sibbil*, b. Aug. 14, 1731; m. Francis Whitmore.

4. *Elias*, b. May. 5, 1734; m. Prudence Savage; d. Jan. 27, 1800.

5. *Aaron*, d. young.

6. *Isaac*, b. Jan. 16, 1741; d. Dec. 8, 1741.

7. *Ruth*, bap. Mar. 27, 1743; m. Dr. John Osborne; d. 1811.

FIFTH GENERATION.

MOSES WHITE, (Isaac[4], Daniel[3], Nathaniel[2], John[1]), eldest son of Deacon Isaac White, was born in Upper Middletown, Aug. 22, 1727. He was a hatter by trade, and spent the greater part of his life in his native place. In old age he removed to Newport, N. H., to a house near that of his son James. He died Oct. 12, 1796. He married, Oct. 12, 1749, Huldah Knowles, of Hartford, who survived him.

CHILDREN.

1. *Huldah*, b. Feb. 10, 1751; m. Nathaniel Eells.

2. *Isaac*, b. Oct. 14, 1752; m. Thankful Clark; d. Jan. 15, 1822.

3. *Ruth*, b. 1754; m. Joseph Ranney; d. Jan. 20, 1824.

4. *Moses*, b. 1757; m. Melitta Porter; d. Nov., 1783.

5. *Roderick*, bap. Mar. 18, 1759.

---

* So the church record. See Appendix II.

6. *James*, bap. Feb. 1, 1761 ; m. Tirzah Taylor ; d. 1813.

7. *Calvin*, b. Dec. 17, 1762 ; successively a Congregational, Presbyterian, and Episcopalian minister ; became a Roman Catholic in 1821 ; m. 1st, Phebe Camp ; 2nd, Jane Mardenbrough.   His second son, Richard Mansfield White, b. May 26, 1797, was the father of Richard Grant White, the editor of Shakespeare, b. May 23, 1821, d. April 8, 1885.   The latter leaves two sons, Richard Mansfield White, b. Dec. 25, 1851, and Stanford White, the well-known architect of New York, b. Nov. 9, 1853.

8. *Roxana*, bap. Sept. 30, 1764 ; m. Stephen Root.

9. *Elisha*, b. Sept. 13, 1766 ; m. Honor Sumner ; d. April 3, 1802.

10. *A child* b. and d. Feb., 1769.

11. *Lucretia*, b. Mar. 5, 1773 ; m. Walter Cooley ; d. Jan. 3, 1849.

SIXTH GENERATION.

ISAAC WHITE (Moses[5], Isaac[4], Daniel[3], Nathaniel[2], John[1]), eldest son of Moses White, was born in Guilford, Conn., Oct. 14, 1752.   He married, Dec. 7, 1775, Thankful Clark, of Southington, who was born Jan. 1, 1760, and died June 27, 1836.   Her father, Col. Joel Clark, was a man of wealth, according to the estimate of the times, and carried on both farming and mercantile business.   When about to leave home at the outbreak of the Revolutionary War to enter the service of his country, he expressed the wish that his two daughters, who were already betrothed, should be married before his departure.   Col. Clark never returned to his family, but died at New York a prisoner of war in 1776.   The daughters carried on his business successfully for some time in their native town.   As the war progressed Isaac White did a seemingly thriving business in furnishing supplies to the Continental Army.   On account of the depreciation of the Continental currency, however, this business ultimately proved disastrous, and diminished greatly the property inherited by his wife.   It was not without difficulty that the debts were paid.   In 1790 Isaac White bade farewell to his friends in Connecticut, and following in the track of his kinsman Hugh White, emigrated to the wilderness of Central New York, settling among the Germans of the Mohawk Valley, about seven miles east of Utica. The following year, having built a log house and raised a crop of grain, he sent for his family, then consisting of his wife and seven children, to come to their new home.   He afterwards removed to Chuckery Corners, in the town of Paris, and finally, about 1815, to Springville, Erie Co., where he died Jan. 15, 1822, aged sixty-nine.

CHILDREN.

1. *Nancy*, b. Jan. 31, 1779; m. Sylvanus Munson; d. Aug. 13, 1849.
2. *Truman*, b. Nov. 8, 1780; m. Betsey Tuthill; d. Jan. 28, 1869.
3. *Francis*, b. July 22, 1782; m. Emma Rushmore; d. Jan. 7, 1858.
4. *Moses*, b. June 30, 1784; m. 1st, Mary Tuthill; 2nd, Sally Cheny; 3d, Mrs. Mary C. Leonard; d.
5. *Isaac*, b. April 27, 1786; d. Aug. 21, 1807.
6. *Roderick*, b. Dec. 8, 1788; m. Lucy Blakeslee; d. Jan. 12, 1877.
7. *Polly*, b. Dec. 22, 1790; m. Samuel Reed Watson; d. Aug. 14, 1881.
8. *Henry*, b. Nov. 8, 1792; d. May, 1793.
9. *Joel*, b. July 2, 1794; m. Phebe Blakeslee; d. Dec., 1869.
10. *Albert*, b. May 19, 1797; m. —— ; d. ——.
11. *Thankful*, b. Sept. 29, 1799; m. Henry Edmonds; d. July 24, 1838.
12. *Almer*, b. Mar. 14, 1802; m. 1st, Ruth Ann Tefft; 2nd, Rebecca Ellinwood; 3d, Cornelia Ellinwood; d.
13. *Frederick*, b. Oct. 24, 1804.

American Ancestry of Lucy Blakeslee.

FIRST GENERATION.

THOMAS BLAKESLEE, born in England in 1615, came to the Colony of Massachusetts Bay in 1635, in the ship Hopewell, Captain Babb, from London. In 1641 he was living in Hartford; in 1643 he removed to New Haven, and in 1645 to Branford. In 1667, 1668, and 1669 he was chosen Deputy to the General Court of Connecticut. He died in 1674 at Boston, whither he had gone on a trading visit, leaving a wife, Susanna Ball.

CHILDREN.

1. *Aaron*, b. 1644; m. 1st, Mary Dodd; 2nd, Mrs. —— Foote.
2. *Moses*, b. Mar. 29, 1650; m. Susanna Bishop.
3. *Miriam*, m. —— Ball.
4. *Abigail*, m. Samuel Pond.

SECOND GENERATION.

AARON BLAKESLEE, (Thomas¹), eldest son of Thomas Blakeslee and Susanna Ball, was born in 1644. He married, 1st, in Feb., 1665, Mary, dau. of Daniel Dodd; 2nd, in 1686, the widow of Robert Foote, of Branford. He is said to have removed to Newark, N. J., after his second marriage.

CHILDREN.

1. *Thomas,* b. 1665; d. Dec. 20, 1692.
2. *Susannah,* b. 1667; m. Ebenezer French; d. Jan. 17, 1728.
3. *Mary,* b. 1668; m. Nath. Allis; d. 1754.
4. *Sarah,* b. 1670.
5. *Samuel,* m. Abigail Finch; d. Oct. 14, 1756.
6. *Hannah,* b. Mar. 5, 1674; d. young.
7. *David,* b. Jan. 9, 1676; m. Mehitabel Evarts; d. May 3, 1712.
8. *Ebenezer,* b. 1677.
9. *Joseph,* b. 1680; m. Mehitabel Keeter; d. Oct. 14, 1704.
10. *Benjamin,* m. Naomi Dudley; d. Dec. 7, 1741.

THIRD GENERATION.

EBENEZER BLAKESLEE, (Aaron[2], Thomas[1]), son of Aaron Blakeslee and Mary Dodd, was born in 1677, and is said to have removed to New Hampshire. A full account of his family is still wanting.

CHILDREN.

1. *Thomas,* b. about 1699; m. Mary ——; d. Jan. 2, 1778.
-. *Joseph,* b. 1713; m. Esther Collins; d. Jan. 19, 1798.

FOURTH GENERATION.

Captain THOMAS BLAKESLEE, (Ebenezer[3], Aaron[2], Thomas[1]), son of Ebenezer Blakeslee, was born about 1699. In 1731 he removed from New Haven to the town of Waterbury. At the time of the Great Revival, 1740, Thomas Blakeslee and ten others, disapproving of the new methods of Mr. Todd, the Congregational minister at Northbury, gained possession of the meeting-house and appropriated it to the services of the Church of England. In 1740 the General Assembly made him Captain of the third company at Waterbury. He died January 2, 1778, leaving a widow, Mary.

CHILDREN.

1. *David,* b. Nov. 2, 1722; m. 1st, Phebe Todd; 2nd, Abigail How.
2. *Reuben,* b. Mar. 9, 1725; m. Mary Ford.
3. *Moses,* b. June 30, 1727; m. Mehitable Allen.
4. *Mary,* b. Sept. 7, 1729; d. 1750.
5. *Submit,* b. 1731; d. 1750.
6. *Experience,* b. Jan. 3, 1735.
7. *Lydia,* b. July 6, 1737; m. Stephen Blakeslee.
8. *Esther,* b. Aug. 6, 1739.
9. *Abigail,* b. Dec. 22, 1741

FIFTH GENERATION.

DAVID BLAKESLEE, (Thomas⁴, Ebenezer³, Aaron², Thomas¹), son of Captain Thomas Blakeslee, was born November 2, 1722. He married 1st, November 29, 1743, Phebe Todd, of New Haven, who died October 4, 1744; 2nd, May 18, 1752, Abigail, dau. of Jonathan How, who died May 6, 1799. In Dec., 1776, he encouraged his son Asa, then twenty years old, to leave Waterbury in order to escape conscription. He was therefore assessed for the support of a soldier, but died before the tax was collected.

CHILDREN.

1. *Thomas*, b. Sept. 17, 1744; m. Lydia Bradley.
2. *Eli*, b. Mar. 22, 1753; m. Lettice Curtis; d. Dec. 6, 1826.
3. *Asa*, b. May 23, 1756; m. Anna Alcott; d. Feb., 1843.
4. *Phebe*, b. June 14, 1758; m. Daniel Harrison.
5. *Ede*, b. Oct. 21, 1760; d. 1771.
6. *Bede*, b. Nov. 9, 1762.
7. *Adnah*, b. Jan. 31, 1765.
8. *David*, b. July 22, 1771; m. 1st, Lucy Seymour; 2nd, Sarah Bailey; d. June 20, 1843.

SIXTH GENERATION.

ELI BLAKESLEE, (David⁵, Thomas⁴, Ebenezer³, Aaron², Thomas¹), son of David Blakeslee and Abigail How, was born March 22, 1753. He married, October 31, 1773, Lettice Curtis. In 1794 he removed with his family to Paris, N. Y. He was one of the founders of the first Episcopal church in Central New York, St. Paul's at Paris Hill, and was its first senior warden. He died Dec. 6, 1826. His wife died May 20, 1830.

CHILDREN.

1. *Prue*, b. June 25, 1775; m. Isaac Ives; d. Aug. 28, 1808.
2. *Orpha*, b. Nov. 3, 1776; m. Samuel Parker.
3. *Charles*, b. Dec. 26, 1778; m. Elizabeth Smith; d. April 20, 1856.
4. *Noah*, b. Feb. 18, 1781; m. Hannah Gaylord; d. Oct. 27, 1845.
5. *Asa*, b. Nov. 6, 1782; m. Annis Tremain; d. Mar. 8, 1860.
6. *Mela*, b. June 4, 1786: m. Buckley Brainard.
7. *Lyman*, b. Mar. 26, 1788; m. Mabel Tremain; d. Oct. 20, 1826.
8. *Ede*, b. April 14, 1790; m. Ansel Brainard.
9. *Mark*, b. Jan. 27, 1792; m. Eunice Judd; d. Sept., 1843.
10. *Phebe*, b. May 27, 1794; m. Joel White; d. about April 1, 1862.
11. *Eli*, b. April 6, 1796; m. Emily Judd.
12. *Lucy*, b. Sept. 1, 1798; m. Roderick White; d. Mar. 15, 1873.

Roderick White and Lucy Blakeslee.

1. RODERICK WHITE, (Isaac[6], Moses[5], Isaac[4], Daniel[3], Nathaniel[2], John[1]), the sixth of the thirteen children of Isaac White and Thankful Clark, was born at Southington, Conn., Dec. 8, 1788, and died at Sauquoit, N. Y., Jan. 12, 1877, having reached a greater age than any of his American ancestors. Although the family removed from Connecticut before he was three years old, he remembered the whipping of a thief at the public whipping post on Southington Green, and some incidents of the long journey by wagon and bateau to the upper Mohawk Valley. His boyhood was spent in the rude but wholesome life of the frontier. From his German neighbors he gained some knowledge of their language, which he always retained. In later life he would tell his children and grandchildren of the bear he met while driving home the cows, of his dangerous fall from a horse, and of being poisoned with wild nuts found in the woods. To these accidents he attributed his short stature, which in manhood was about five feet one and one half inch. His scanty school privileges in childhood were supplemented by two winter terms at the Fairfield Academy, and he taught school at least one term. For several years he was a merchant's clerk at Newport, Herkimer Co., N. Y. At the age of twenty-one, becoming convinced that his health required active, out-of-door labor, he chose the carpenter's trade, which he followed during the rest of his life. He became muscular and hardy, and would never acknowledge himself sick or tired. He usually worked without a hat and knew nothing of headache by experience.

He purchased of Joseph Hall, April 29, 1815, six acres of woodland and a home-lot of five acres. In the log house upon this lot lived Eli Blakeslee and his family in the summer of 1816. Here occurred the wedding of Roderick White and Lucy Blakeslee, July 5, 1816. Upon this Home-lot, in a house which he built later, their children were born and brought up, and

here the Golden Wedding was celebrated July 5, 1866, in the presence of the ten surviving children and many grandchildren. He conveyed the Home-lot by deed to his son Aaron, April 25, 1874. For many years he was a member of the Methodist Episcopal church, but afterwards joined the Freewill Baptist denomination on account of his sympathy with the advanced views held by this body of Christians regarding the abolition of slavery. His constant habit was industry, and both father and mother were faithful in the discipline of their household. At the age of fifty he gave up the use of tobacco for example's sake, and none of his sons ever fell into that snare. Vivacious, agile, self-opinioned, and eccentric, he was a man of keen sense and sound religious principles. By the younger generation he is remembered as the kindest and most companionable of grandfathers.

LUCY BLAKESLEE, dau. of Eli Blakeslee and Lettice Curtis, was born in the town of Paris, Oneida Co., N. Y., Sept. 1, 1798, and died Mar. 15, 1873. She was the youngest of a family of six sons and six daughters. She inherited from her parents a strong constitution, and was taught both by precept and example all that is implied in the terms industry, economy, integrity, and the fear of God. She enjoyed no educational advantages except those of the common school ; but having an active mind and remarkable memory, she acquired a store of information above most of her associates. Until her marriage she had rarely left the neighborhood of her home, but was devoted to domestic pursuits in her father's house, becoming skillful in spinning and weaving of both linen and woolen, for at that time all the clothing as well as the bedding for the family was home-made. Married in her eighteenth year, she settled with her husband in her native town, one and one-fourth mile north of Paris Hill. Here they lived fifty-six years. In the autumn of 1872, suffering somewhat from the feebleness of age, they consented to leave the old home to which they were strongly attached, and go to the village of Sauquoit, only four miles distant, to spend the remnant of life with their daughter Phebe. The aged mother seemed cheerful and happy in her new home, but after a few months, weakened by partial paralysis, she fell to the floor, dislocating her left hip. Her old physician, Dr. Larrabee, of Paris Hill, assisted by Dr. Bishop, of Sauquoit, replaced the injured bones and gave her the most

faithful attention, as also did her children ; but after about six weeks of suffering she heard the Welcome for which she longed, and was at rest.   Having done well as daughter, wife, and mother, neighbor, friend, and Christian, she was known only to be loved, and departed lamented by all, especially by her children, who '' arise up and call her blessed.''   After four years of patient waiting, marked only by gradual decay of his physical powers, Roderick White rejoined the greatly missed companion of his youth.

CHILDREN.

2+. *Leonard White*, b. May 30, 1817 ; m. Clarissa Cone ; d. June 29, 1878.

3+. *Moses Clark White*, b. July 24, 1819 ; m. 1st, Jane I. Atwater ; 2nd, Mary Seely.

4+. *Lois White*, b. Feb. 7, 1822 ; m. George M. Tooley ; d. Jan. 12, 1882.

5+. *Aaron White*, b. Sept. 18, 1824 ; m. Isadore Maria Haight.

6+. *Joseph White*, b. Apr. 10, 1827 ; m. 1st, Susan E. Beebee ; 2nd, Lucy E. Lewis.

7. *Martha White*, b. Apr. 16, 1829 ; m. Aug. 1, 1857, Alva Hotchkiss Long, son of Jeremiah B. C. Long and Sarah Rouse, who was b. at Oran, Onondaga Co., N. Y., Dec. 10, 1826, and d. at his home near Chittenango, N. Y., Jan. 5, 1892.   Both were educated at Cazenovia Seminary and taught many years in various public schools of Central New York.   In 1860–61 they taught at Pine Bluff, Ark.   Mrs. Martha White Long resides at Cazenovia, N. Y.

8+. *Jennette White*, b. July 6, 1831 ; m. Franklin Lohnes.

9. *Eli White*, b. Nov. 15, 1833 ; d. Mar. 17, 1840.

10+. *Phebe White*, b. July 1, 1836 ; m. Isaac M. Maltby.

11+. *Laura White*, b. Dec. 23, 1838 ; m. William A. Hopper.

12+. *Frederick Samson White*, b. Feb. 2, 1845 ; m. 1st, Margaret M. Brown ; 2nd, Frances Ann Bracken.

Descendants of Roderick White.

2. LEONARD WHITE* (Roderick⁷), eldest son of Roderick White and Lucy Blakeslee, was born in Paris*, Oneida Co., N. Y., May 30, 1817. He married at Jefferson, O., Oct. 10, 1838, Clarissa Cone of Paris, N. Y., dau. of Caleb Cone and Clarissa Sackett, who was born Aug. 19, 1817. During the winter of 1838-39 they lived at Medina, O., returning to Paris, N. Y., in the spring of 1839. In the fall of that year he removed to Oneida, where he taught a school of the Oneida Indians. In 1840 he removed to Vernon, and in 1841 to Cazenovia, where he lived until 1869. In this year he removed to Auburn, N. Y., where he died June 29, 1878. He was converted and joined the Methodist Episcopal church at Paris Hill in 1834, was licensed as an Exhorter in 1838, was licensed to preach June 26, 1841, and was a Licensed Preacher of the Methodist Episcopal church until his death. He worked most of his life at his trade as a master carpenter. He was quite eccentric, but a man of sterling integrity, and so strictly honest that if any one came in to talk with him when he was at work, he would note the time spent, and deduct it from his day's bill for labor. When he finally had to quit work by reason of his fatal illness, he could say, that he did not owe a cent in the world. Although not popular, he was always respected in the communities in which he lived. He trained up his five children in the fear of the Lord, and was always an earnest worker in the Christian Church.

CHILDREN.

13+. *Clarissa Amelia White*, b. Jan. 17, 1840; m. Jerome B. Allen.
14+. *Roderick White*, b. Dec. 14, 1841; m. Mary F. Steele.
15+. *Huldah White*, b. Oct. 12, 1843; m. David H. Fay.
16+. *Oscar White*, b. July 20, 1845; m. Elizabeth Jane Roberts.
17+. *Ossian Charles White*, b. June 7, 1847; m. Catherine Ann Dean.

---

*Roderick White's Home-lot is in the south-east part of the town of Kirkland, which was set off from Paris in 1827.

3. MOSES CLARK WHITE[1], (Roderick[1]), son of Roderick White and Lucy Blakeslee, was born in Paris, N. Y., July 24, 1819. In November, 1840, he entered Cazenovia Seminary. In February, 1842, he entered Wesleyan University, at Middletown, Conn., and graduated third in rank in his class in 1845. In 1845–46 he pursued theological and medical studies in Yale University, besides preaching in New Haven and Milford. He was ordained Elder in the Methodist Episcopal church Mar. 30, 1847, and having been appointed missionary to China, sailed from Boston April 15 of that year. From 1847 to 1853 he was a missionary and physician in Foo-Chow. He had charge there of a dispensary, had an extensive medical and surgical practice among the Chinese, and obtained great favor among all ranks of the people. In 1851 he published a translation of the Gospel of Matthew in the colloquial language of Foo-Chow, which was the first book ever published in that dialect. In 1853 he returned to the United States and established himself in New Haven as a physician. In 1857 he was appointed Lecturer on Microscopy in the Medical Department of Yale College, and in 1867 Professor of Microscopy and Pathology. He is now senior professor in the department. He served as Secretary of the Connecticut Medical Society from 1864 to 1876. In 1856 he published an "Introduction to the Study of the Colloquial Language of Foo-Chow." He assisted largely in the preparation and publication of "Silliman's Physics," and wrote the chapter on optics. He revised and edited the second edition of Porter's Chemistry. He gave instruction in Botany from 1861 to 1864 in the Sheffield Scientific School, and from 1869 to 1875 lectured in the Wesleyan University on the microscopical structure of plants and animals. He married 1st, Mar. 13, 1847, Jane Isabel Atwater, of Homer, N. Y., dau. of Ezra Atwater, who was born Aug. 26, 1822, and died at Foo-Chow, May 25, 1848; 2nd, July 14, 1851, Mary Seely, dau. of Joseph Owen Seely, of South Onondaga, N. Y., who was born May 13, 1821, and died at New Haven, Mar. 19, 1887.

CHILDREN.

18. *George White*, b. May 24, 1852; d. May 25, 1852.

19. *Caryl Fenelon Seely White*, b. April 5, 1856. He received the degree of M.D. from Yale University in 1881, and is a physician in New Haven, Conn.

20+. *Eugene Henry White*, b. Sept. 4, 1862; m. Minnie H. Tryon.

4. LOIS WHITE⁴, (Roderick¹), daughter of Roderick White and Lucy Blakeslee, was born in Paris, N. Y., Feb. 7, 1822, and married, Dec. 24, 1844, George Minott Tooley, son of Peter Tooley and Lucretia Wheeler Brigham, who was born at Hanover, Oneida Co., N. Y., Aug. 27, 1818. They settled in Palermo, Oswego Co., N. Y., where she died Jan. 12, 1882, after a very short illness from apoplexy. George M. Tooley is a farmer at Clifford, Oswego Co., N. Y.

CHILDREN.

21. *Jennette Lucretia Tooley*, b. Sept. 27, 1845 ; d. Aug. 15, 1848.

22. *Lucy Jane Tooley*, b. July 14, 1847 ; m. July 2, 1865, Houghton Kellogg Andrews, son of Robert Kellogg Andrews and Esther Tucker, who was b. at Clyde, N. Y., Dec. 13, 1845. H. K. Andrews was engaged in farming in Oswego and Otsego counties until 1879. Since that time he has been a carpenter and painter at Antwerp, Jefferson Co., N. Y. They have

    85. *Hattie Marion Andrews*, b. at South Valley, Otsego Co., N. Y., Feb. 2, 1869 ; educated at Ives Seminary ; teacher at Antwerp, N. Y.

    86. *Minnie Bell Andrews*, b. at Hastings, N. Y., Apr. 2, 1872 ; d. Aug. 11, 1873.

    87. *Ervin Houghton Andrews*, b. at Palermo, N. Y., Dec. 22, 1873 ; educated at Ives Seminary ; mechanic at Antwerp, N. Y.

23. *Martha Elizabeth Tooley*, b. Nov. 17, 1849 ; educated at the Oswego Normal School ; a teacher.

24. *Laura Maria Tooley*, b. Apr. 26, 1853 ; d. Oct. 18, 1853.

25. *Mary Louisa Tooley*, b. Nov. 2, 1854 ; a teacher.

26. *George Addison Tooley*, b. Nov. 4, 1857 ; d. Sept. 11, 1859.

27. *Jennie Tooley*, b. June 28, 1859 ; d. June 28, 1859.

28. *Jessie Tooley*, b. June 28, 1859 ; d. Aug. 12, 1859.

29. *Minott Fremont Tooley*, b. Apr. 14, 1861 ; educated at Mexico Academy ; m. June 29, 1888, Maude Bridella Gilman, dau. of Levi L. Gilman and Rosa Adelia Jennings, of Palermo, N. Y., who was b. Nov. 6, 1868. They have

    88. *Queenia Rose Tooley*, b. at Clifford, N. Y., Apr. 24, 1889.

    89. *Minnie Lois Tooley*, b. June 5, 1892.

30. *Elmer Baxter Tooley*, b. June 6, 1863 ; educated at Mexico Academy ; teacher at Goshen, Conn., 1887-88 ; farmer at Palermo, N. Y., 1888-92.

31. *James Austin Tooley*, b. July 3, 1865 ; educated at Mexico Academy and Hamilton College, from which he received the degree of A.B., 1890 ; teacher in the Cayuga Lake Military Academy at Aurora, N. Y., 1890-92.

5. AARON WHITE⁴, (Roderick¹), son of Roderick White and Lucy Blakeslee, was born in Paris, N. Y., Sept 18, 1824. He was educated at Cazenovia Seminary and Wesleyan University, from which he received the degree of A.B. in 1852 and A.M. in

1855. He was a teacher in Flushing Female Institute, 1852–53; teacher of mathematics in Cazenovia Seminary, 1853–66; principal of Sauquoit Academy, 1866–69; teacher in Cazenovia Seminary, 1869–70; principal of Canastota Union Free School and Academy, 1870–79; principal of White's English and Classical School at Oneida, 1879–80; teacher in Cazenovia Seminary, 1880 to the present time. · He married, Apr. 6, 1859, Isadore Maria Haight, of Cazenovia, N. Y., dau. of William Henry Haight and Cornelia Cushing, who was born Mar. 13, 1835.

CHILDREN.

32. *Cornelia Cushing White*, b. at Cazenovia, N. Y., Feb. 3, 1860; a graduate of Cazenovia Seminary in 1881.

33. *Henry Seely White*, b. at Cazenovia, May 20, 1861; m. Oct. 28, 1890, Mary Willard Gleason, of Hartford, Conn., dau. of Frederick Gleason and Martha Willard, who was b. Oct. 29, 1861. Henry S. White prepared for college at the Cazenovia Seminary; graduated from Wesleyan University with the degree of A.B. in 1882; was assistant in the Wesleyan University Astronomical Observatory, 1882–83; teacher in the Centenary Collegiate Institute at Hackettstown, N. J., 1883–84; tutor in Wesleyan University, 1884-87; student of higher mathematics at the University of Göttingen, 1887–90. He received the degree of Ph.D. from the University of Göttingen in 1890, presenting as his inaugural dissertation a treatise upon Abelian Integrals. He was Assistant in mathematics at Clark University, Worcester, Mass., 1890–92. In the summer of 1892 he was apppointed Associate Professor of Mathematics in Northwestern University at Evanston, Ill.

34. *Lucy Blakeslee White*, b. at Sauquoit, N. Y., Feb. 8, 1869; prepared for college at Cazenovia Seminary; graduated with the degree of A.B. at Wellesley College, 1891; teacher in the State Normal School at New Britain, Conn., 1891–92.

6. JOSEPH WHITE[3], (Roderick[1]), son of Roderick White and Lucy Blakeslee, was born in Paris, N. Y., April 10, 1827. He married 1st, Apr. 20, 1853, Susan Elizabeth Beebee, dau. of Jason Beebee and Nancy Terry, who was born at Newport, N. Y., Aug. 29, 1826, and died at Utica, Nov. 8, 1886; 2nd, Aug. 15, 1888, Lucy Electra Lewis, of Kirkland, dau. of Elisha Chauncey Lewis and Electra Brown, who was born Apr. 18, 1850. He purchased a part of his father's home-lot near Paris Hill, built a dwelling, and lived there until May, 1863, when he removed with his family to Utica. He was for some years engaged in the planing mill business, and is now a manufacturer of cigar boxes.

35+. *Andrew Curtis White*, b. Nov. 25, 1854; m. Minnie Langworthy.

36+. *Albert Terry White*, b. July 10, 1856; m. Charlotte Boyle Hopkins.

(BY ADOPTION.)

37. *Olley Ettna While*, b. Aug. 19, 1890.

8. JENNETE WHITE[8], (Roderick[7]), dau. of Roderick White and Lucy Blakeslee, was born in Kirkland, N. Y., July 6, 1831. She married, Nov. 2, 1853, Franklin Lohnes, son of Sebastian Lohnes and Eve Bulson, who was born in Lee, Oneida Co., N. Y., Mar. 3, 1832. In November, 1858, they removed from Floyd, N. Y., to Frankford, Ontario, where they still reside.

CHILDREN.

38. *Mary Eliza Lohnes*, b. Jan. 17, 1855; m. at Frankford, Dec. 28, 1874, George Washington Potter, son of Rowlin Potter and Mary Rikely, who was b. May 12, 1848, at Frankford. He is a mason and lives at Frankford. They have :

    93. *Zoa May Potter*, b. Jan. 17, 1878.

    94. *Louisa Potter*, b. June 12, 1880.

    95. *Jennette Potter*, b. July 3, 1882.

    96. *Alice Eveline Potter*, b. Aug. 26, 1887; d. Jan. 3, 1888.

39. *Harriet Eveline* (commonly called *Eva*) *Lohnes*, b. Oct. 7, 1856; m. at Frankford, Dec. 29, 1874, William Henry Weese, son of Benjamin Weese and Elizabeth Dempsy, who was b. in Prince Edward, Dec. 3, 1847. He is a policeman at Saginaw, Mich., where they reside. They have :

    97. *Franklin Chauncy Weese*, b. Mar. 3, 1877.

    98. *Walter Weese*, born April 25, 1880.

    99. *Nettie May Weese*, b. May 6, 1884.

    100. *Myrtle Weese*, b. Feb. 27, 1890.

40. *Jennie Emogene Lohnes*, b. Aug. 11, 1858; m. at Chittenango, N. Y., Mar. 16, 1881, Ambrose Spencer Long, son of Alva Hotchkiss Long by his first wife, Mary Janet Sweet, who was b. Oct. 13, 1854. He has been a farmer; is now a fireman in the service of the New York Central R. R. They reside at East Syracuse, N. Y. They have :

    101. *Herbert Arthur Long*, b. Dec. 28, 1881.

    102. *Clara Annie Long*, b. Mar. 23, 1883.

    103. *Edith Adaline Long*, b. Nov. 14, 1884.

    104. *Emory Ambrose Long*, b. July 17, 1886.

41. *Anne Estalia Lohnes*, b. Aug. 4, 1861; m. at Frankford, Sept. 4, 1878, Clarence Hendricks, son of Hiram Hendricks and Mary Ann McFaul, who was b. in Murray, Ont., Aug. 19, 1858. He is a farmer in Murray, Ont. They have :

    105. *Walter Elwood Hendricks*, born Aug. 19, 1879.

    106. *Elura Hendricks*, b. Jan. 28, 1881.

107. *Albert Jerome Hendricks*, b. Mar. 9, 1885.

108. *Clara Hendricks*, b. Sept. 8, 1887.

109. *Leonard Maxwell Hendricks*, b. July 7, 1889.

110. *Eva Edna Hendricks*, born Sept. 15, 1891.

42. *Emory Edward Lohnes*, b. Sept. 4, 1864; m. at Saginaw, Mich., Sept. 4, 1888, Jennie May Osborne, dau. of D. W. Osborne, of Saginaw, Mich., who was born June 24, 1865. E. E. Lohnes is General Secretary of the Young Men's Christian Association at Alpena, Mich. They have:

111. *Neta Osborne Lohnes*, b. April 18, 1890.

43. *Florence Augusta Lohnes*, b. July 29, 1869; m. Jan. 10, 1887, Herbert M. Faul, son of James Faul, of Murray, Ont., who was b. June 16, 1859. He is a teacher and lives at Leamington, Essex Co., Ont. They have:

112. *Earl Faul*, b. July 16, 1888.

44. *Charles Albert Lohnes*, b. Aug. 2, 1872.

45. *Gilbert Wesley Lohnes*, b. Sept. 16, 1877.

10. PHEBE WHITE[9], (Roderick[7]), dau. of Roderick White and Lucy Blakeslee, was born in Kirkland, N. Y., July 1, 1836. She was educated at Cazenovia Seminary and was a teacher until her marriage, March 23, 1869, to Isaac Morris Maltby, son of Morris Maltby and Sybil Todd, who was born in Paris, N. Y., Jan. 4, 1807, and died Jan. 5, 1891. They lived at Sauquoit until April 1, 1883, when they removed to Cazenovia.

CHILDREN.

46. *Jessie Laura Maltby*, b. Nov. 25, 1871; a graduate of Cazenovia Seminary; is a teacher.

47. *Morris White Maltby*, b. Mar. 28, 1874; is a telegraphic operator in New York City.

11. LAURA WHITE[9], (Roderick[7]), dau. of Roderick White and Lucy Blakeslee, was born in Kirkland, N. Y., Dec. 23, 1838. She was educated at Cazenovia Seminary. She married, Sept. 5, 1860, William Avery Hopper, son of John Hopper and Catherine Schegel, who was born at Peekskill, N. Y., July 30, 1837. He is a farmer. They have lived at Chittenango, N. Y., 1860–62; at Waterloo, N. Y., 1862–67; at Pithole and Pleasantville, Pa., 1867–70; at Greeley, Col., 1870; at Fremont, Neb., 1870–72; at Downs, Osborne Co., Kas., 1872 to the present time.

CHILDREN.

48. *George Edward Hopper*, b. at Chittenango, N. Y., Nov. 16, 1861. He graduated from the Kansas State Agricultural College in 1885, and received the degree of M. Sc. in 1890. He is a contractor and builder at Manhattan,

Kas. He m., June 4, 1882, at Alma, Kas., Margery McElroy, dau. of Thomas R. McElroy and Elizabeth Wilson, who was born at Collingwood, Canada, Sept. 12, 1862. They have

113. *Agnes Laura Hopper*, b. July 23, 1885.
114. *William Hopper*, b. June 21, 1887.
115. *Frederick Hopper*, b. May 25, 1889.
116. *Joseph Hopper*, b. July 2, 1891.

49. *Lucy Blakeslee Hopper*, b. at Waterloo, N. Y., Feb. 20, 1863; m. at Downs, Kas., Oct. 8, 1882, Alexander Getty, son of Samuel A. Getty and Sarah M. Brown, who was b. at Armaugh, Pa., Feb. 11, 1857. He is a farmer at Downs, Kas. They have

117. *Edward Albert Getty*, b. Sept. 15, 1883.
118. *Laura Mercy Getty*, b. Nov. 2. 1887.

50. *Maria Crasson Hopper*, b. at Waterloo, N. Y., Oct. 9, 1865; graduated from the Kansas State Agricultural College in 1886; m. Dec. 30, 1888, Edward Louis Getty, son of Samuel A. Getty and Sarah M. Brown, who was born at Bell's Mills, Pa., Dec. 30, 1860. He is a merchant's clerk at Greenleaf, Kas. They have

119. *Richard William Getty*, b. at Downs, Kas., Nov. 28, 1889.

12. FREDERICK SAMSON WHITE[3], (Roderick[1]), son of Roderick White and Lucy Blakeslee, was born in Kirkland, N. Y., Feb. 2, 1845. Sept. 15, 1862, he enlisted in Company A, 146th New York Volunteers, at Utica, N. Y., and served continuously until July 28, 1865, when the regiment was discharged at Syracuse, N. Y. He received a commission as second lieutenant on the day of his discharge. He is an architect and stair builder in Cleveland, O. He married, 1st, Sept. 4, 1866, Margaret M. Brown, b. Nov. 4. 1846; 2nd, May 23, 1878, Frances Ann Bracken, dau. of William Bracken and Isabella Thompson, who was born at Florencecourt, near Enniskillen, Ireland, Dec. 24, 1846.

CHILDREN (BY FIRST MARRIAGE).

51. *Jennette White*, b. at Utica, N. Y., Sept. 5, 1868; d. Feb. 13, 1869.
52. *Frederick White*, b. at Utica, N. Y., May 21, 1870; d. Jan. 21, 1871.
53. *Mary Louisa White*, b. in New York City, Jan. 14, 1873.

(BY SECOND MARRIAGE.)

54. *John Arthur White*, b. at Cleveland, O., May 27, 1880; d. July 15, 1880.
55. *Eli White*, b. at Cleveland, O., Nov. 14, 1882.
56. *Andrew Bracken White*, b. at Cleveland, O., Dec. 21, 1884.

NINTH GENERATION.

13. CLARISSA AMELIA WHITE[9], (Leonard[8], Roderick[1]), dau. of Leonard White and Clarissa Cone, was born Jan. 17, 1840. She m. at Cazenovia, N. Y., Oct. 28, 1863, Jerome Bonaparte Allen, son of Samuel Allen, who was born at Brookfield, Madison Co., N. Y., Oct. 9, 1830. He was a cabinet maker, and died at Cazenovia, Feb. 20, 1892.

CHILDREN.

57. *Charles Edward Allen*, b. at Cazenovia, Feb. 28, 1865 ; is a cabinet maker at Cazenovia ; m. Sept. 15, 1888, Anna Matthews, dau. of Owen and Sarah Matthews, who was b. Mar. 3, 1872. They have
  120. *Charles Edward Allen, Jr.*, b. Aug. 30, 1889.
58. *George Maxon Allen*, b. Apr. 22, 1867.
59. *Ellen Minerva Allen*, b. Jan. 28, 1869 ; m. Aug. 22, 1889, William H. Manning, of Cazenovia, a railroad brakeman. They have
  121. *Olie Manning*, b. Dec. 15, 1891.
60. *Arthur Jerome Allen*, b. June 15, 1871 ; d. July 15, 1872.
61. *Almon Emory Allen*, b. June 14, 1873 ; d. Dec. 23, 1873.
62. *Almina Elvenah Allen*, b. June 14, 1873 ; d. Aug. 28, 1874.
63. *Mary Levanche Allen*, b. Aug. 11, 1875.
64. *Adelbert William Allen*, b. June 28, 1879 ; d. July 17, 1880.

14. RODERICK WHITE[9], (Leonard[8], Roderick[1]), son of Leonard White and Clarissa Cone, was born Dec. 14, 1841. He enlisted as a private in Company E, 8th Regiment N. Y. V., Cavalry, Capt. Wm. H. Healy, Oct. 3, 1861, and re-enlisted in the field, Dec. 1, 1863. He was taken prisoner near Ream's Station, Va., on what is known as the "Wilson Raid," June 29, 1864. He was a prisoner of war eight months at Salisbury, N. C., Andersonville, Ga., Millen, Ga., and Florence, S. C., and was paroled Feb. 28, 1865. He participated in forty-four engagements. He received his discharge as sergeant at Cloud's Mills, Va., June 27, 1865. He is a carpenter and has lived for many years at Auburn, N. Y. He was elected School Commissioner of the city of Auburn in May, 1890. He married at Sauquoit, N. Y., July 27, 1865, Mary Frances Steele, dau. of Thomas Steele and Ellen Kenna, who was born in County Longford, Ireland, Dec. 19, 1844.

CHILDREN.

65+. *Mary Ellen White*, b. at Cazenovia, N. Y., Nov. 17, 1867 ; m. George King.
66. *Jennie May White*, b. at Cazenovia, Nov. 18, 1868.

67. *Hattie Louisa White*, b. at Auburn, Aug. 16, 1870.
68. *Carrie Blanche White*, b. at Auburn, Mar. 24, 1875.
69. *Frederick William White*, b. at Auburn, Sept. 10, 1876.
70. *Albert Grant White*, b. at Auburn, May. 15, 1879.

15. HULDAH WHITE⁸, (Leonard², Roderick¹), dau. of Leonard White and Clarissa Cone, was born Oct. 12, 1843. She m. July 12, 1865, David Henry Fay, son of Leonard Fay and Susan E. Hughs, who was b. at Cazenovia, N. Y., Oct. 12, 1841. He enlisted as a private, Oct. 12, 1861, in Company G, 81st N. Y. V. He was wounded at the battle of Fair Oaks, Va., May 31, 1862, and was discharged at Yorktown, Va., Sept. 3. 1862. They reside at Downs, Kas.

CHILDREN.

71. *William Henry Fay*, b. at Leavenworth, Kas., May 26, 1866.
72. *Edward David Fay*, b. at Wisner, Neb., Oct. 5, 1869.
73. *Frank Leonard Fay*, b. at Wisner, Neb., May 20, 1871 ; d. June 1, 1871.
74. *Arthur Leonard Fay*, b. at Wisner, Neb., July 26, 1872.
75. *Clara Edith Fay*, b. at Wisner, Neb., Sept. 5, 1874.
76. *John Albert Fay*, b. at Wisner, Neb., April 6, 1877.
77. *Fanny Maria Fay*, b. at Portis, Kas., Dec. 24, 1879.
78. *Gertrude Lucinda Fay*, b. at Portis, Kas., June 19, 1882.

16. OSCAR WHITE⁸, (Leonard², Roderick¹), son of Leonard White and Clarissa Cone, was born at Cazenovia, N. Y., July 20, 1845. He enlisted in Company H, 2d N. Y. V., Heavy Artillery, March 10, 1862. He took part in forty-two engagements, including the second battle of Bull Run, Spottsylvania Court House, and Cold Harbor. He was discharged Oct. 10, 1865. He is a carpenter at Auburn, N. Y. He married at Canastota, N. Y., March 24, 1868, Elizabeth Jane Roberts, dau. of Robert E. Roberts and Hannah Jones, who was born in Wales, June 14, 1848.

CHILDREN.

79. *Leonard Robert White*, b. at Syracuse, N. Y., May 29, 1876.
80. *George White*, b. at Syracuse, N. Y., May 20, 1879 ; d. May 22, 1879.
81. *Mabel Hannah White*, b. at Auburn, N. Y., Sept. 12, 1880.

17. OSSIAN CHARLES WHITE⁸, (Leonard², Roderick¹), son of Leonard White and Clarissa Cone, was born at Cazenovia, N. Y., June 7, 1847. He enlisted in the 22nd N. Y. V., Cavalry, Dec. 30, 1863. He was taken prisoner at White Post, Va., Aug.

19, 1864, and was held a prisoner of war at Front Royal, Winchester, Stanton, and Libby Prison. He was paroled from Libby Prison in October, 1864, and was exchanged under cartel of Nov. 24, 1864. He joined his regiment at Winchester in January, 1865, and was discharged Aug. 9, 1865. He is a photographic artist at Auburn, N. Y. He married, Nov. 6, 1865, Catherine Ann Dean, of Auburn, dau. of Robert B. Dean and Eliza Atkins, who was born May 1, 1848

CHILDREN.

82. *Robert Leonard White*, b. at Cazenovia, N. Y., Nov. 11, 1866; d. at Auburn, Oct. 3, 1869.

83. *Charles Dean White*, b. at Auburn, Sept. 28, 1880.

20. EUGENE HENRY WHITE[9], (Moses C.[8], Roderick[7]), son of Moses Clark White and Mary Seely, was born at New Haven, Conn., Sept. 4. 1862. He is a hardware manufacturer at New Haven, Conn. He married, June 26, 1888, Minnie Harriet Tryon, dau. of Capt. John Wesley Tryon and Abbie Jane Brown, who was born at East Hampton, Conn., Dec. 29, 1862. They have

84. *Jessie May White*, b. June 14, 1891.

35. ANDREW CURTIS WHITE[9], (Joseph[8], Roderick[7]), son of Joseph White and Susan Elizabeth Beebee, was born in Kirkland, N. Y., Nov. 25, 1854. He prepared for college at the Utica Free Academy, and is a graduate of Hamilton College, in the class of 1881. In 1881-82 he was a teacher in the Cayuga Lake Academy, at Aurora, N. Y. Since that time he has lived in Ithaca, N. Y. ; 1882-85, pursued philogical studies in Cornell University, receiving the degree of Ph.D. in 1885 ; 1885-86, Instructor in Latin in Cornell University ; 1886-89, Instructor in Latin, Greek, and Ancient History in Cornell University ; 1889 to the present time, Assistant Librarian in the Cornell University Library. He married, June 25, 1890, Minnie Langworthy, of Utica, N. Y., dau. of Rev. John Martin Langworthy and Diana Abigail Dennison, who was born at Prospect, Oneida Co., N. Y., Aug. 22, 1859. They have

90. *John Langworthy White*, b. at Ithaca, N. Y., April 29, 1892.

36. ALBERT TERRY WHITE[9], (Joseph[8], Roderick[7]), son of Joseph White and Susan Elizabeth Beebee, was born in Kirkland,

N. Y., July 10, 1856. He is a graduate of the Utica Free Academy in the class of 1874. He is a mechanic at Utica, N. Y. He married, Dec. 17, 1879, Charlotte Boyle Hopkins, of Utica, eldest dau. of William Edwin Hopkins and Sophia Lucy Curtis, who was born at Utica, Jan. 24, 1857.

CHILDREN.

91. *Albert Hopkins White*, b. at Utica, June 11, 1881.
92. *Esther Evangeline White*, b. at Utica, Mar. 9, 1883.

TENTH GENERATION.

65. MARY ELLEN WHITE[10], (Roderick[9], Leonard[8], Roderick[7]), eldest dau. of Roderick White and Mary Frances Steele, was born at Cazenovia, N. Y., Nov. 17, 1867. She married at Auburn, N. Y., Mar. 24, 1887, George King, son of Marquis King, who died May 29, 1889.

CHILDREN.

122. *Frances Adelaide King*, b. in Owasco, Cayuga Co., N. Y., Feb. 3, 1888.
123. *Clarence Roderick King*, b. at Auburn, N. Y., Aug. 3, 1889.

1605421

APPENDIX I.

ANALYTICAL TABLE OF DESCENT.

FIRST GENERATION.

John White, 1600—1684.   Thomas Blakeslee, 1615—1674.

SECOND GENERATION.

Nathaniel White, 1629—1711. Aaron Blakeslee, 1644—

THIRD GENERATON.

Daniel White, 1661—1739.   Ebenezer Blakeslee, 1677—

FOURTH GENERATION.

Isaac White, 1696—1768.   Thomas Blakeslee, 1699—1778.

FIFTH GENERATION.

Moses White, 1727—1796.   David Blakeslee, 1722—

SIXTH GENERATION.

Isaac White, 1752—1822.   Eli Blakeslee, 1753—1826.

SEVENTH GENERATION.

1. Roderick White, 1788—1877 = Lucy Blakeslee, 1798—1873.

[The descendants of Roderick White and Lucy Blakeslee are grouped (1) by generations, (2) by families, the number at the left of the brace being in every instance that of the immediate ancestor. The asterisk (*) indicates decease.]

EIGHTH GENERATION.

1.
2. *Leonard White, 1817–1878.
3. Moses Clark White, 1819.
4. *Lois White (Tooley), 1822–1882.
5. Aaron White, 1824.
6. Joseph White, 1827.
7. Martha White (Long), 1829.
8. Jennette White (Lohnes), 1831.
9. *Eli White, 1833–1840.
10. Phebe White (Maltby), 1836.
11. Laura White (Hopper), 1838.
12. Frederick Samson White, 1845.

NINTH GENERATION.

2.
13. Clarissa Amelia White (Allen), 1840.
14. Roderick White, 1841.
15. Huldah White (Fay), 1843.
16. Oscar White, 1845.
17. Ossian Charles White, 1847.

18. *George White, 1852-1852.
3.
19. Caryl Fenelon Seely White, 1856.
20. Eugene Henry White, 1862.

21. *Jennette Lucretia Tooley, 1845-1848.
22. Lucy Jane Tooley (Andrews), 1847.
23. Martha Elizabeth Tooley, 1849.
4.
24. *Laura Maria Tooley, 1853-1853.
25. Mary Louisa Tooley, 1854.
26. George Addison Tooley, 1857.
27. *Jennie Tooley, 1859-1859.
28. *Jessie Tooley, 1859-1859
29. Minott Fremont Tooley, 1861.
30. Elmer Baxter Tooley, 1863.
31. James Austin Tooley, 1865.

5.
32. Cornelia Cushing White, 1860.
33. Henry Seely White, 1861.
34. Lucy Blakeslee White, 1869.

NINTH GENERATION.

(*Continued.*)

6. 35. Andrew Curtis White, 1854.
36. Albert Terry White, 1856.
37. Olley Ettua White, 1890.

8. 38. Mary Eliza Lohnes (Potter), 1855.
39. Harriet Eveline Lohnes (Weese), 1856.
40. Jennie Emogene Lohnes (Long), 1858.
41. Anne Estatia Lohnes (Hendricks), 1861.
42. Emory Edward Lohnes, 1864.
43. Florence Augusta Lohnes (Faul), 1869.
44. Charles Albert Lohnes, 1872.
45. Gilbert Wesley Lohnes, 1877.

10. 46. Jessie Laura Maltby, 1871.
47. Morris White Maltby, 1874.

11. 48. George Edward Hopper, 1861.
49. Lucy Blakeslee Hopper (Getty), 1863.
50. Maria Crasson Hopper (Getty), 1865.

12. 51. *Jennette White, 1868-1869.
52. *Frederick White, 1870-1871.
53. Mary Louisa White, 1873.
54. *John Arthur White, 1880-1880.
55. Eli White, 1882.
56. Andrew Bracken White, 1884.

TENTH GENERATION.

13. 57. Charles Edward Allen, 1865.
58. George Maxon Allen, 1867.
59. Ellen Minerva Allen (Manning), 1869.
60. *Arthur Jerome Allen, 1871-1872.
61. *Almon Emory Allen, 1873-1873.
62. *Almina Elvenah Allen, 1873-1874.
63. Mary Levanche Allen, 1875.
64. Adelbert William Allen, 1879-1880.

14. 65. Mary Ellen White (King), 1867.
66. Jennie May White, 1868.
67. Hattie Louisa White, 1870.
68. Carrie Blanche White, 1875.
69. Frederick William White, 1876.
70. Albert Grant White, 1879.

15. 71. William Henry Fay, 1866.
72. Edward David Fay, 1869.
73. *Frank Leonard Fay, 1871-1871.
74. Arthur Leonard Fay, 1872.
75. Clara Edith Fay, 1874.
76. John Albert Fay, 1877.
77. Fanny Maria Fay, 1879.
78. Gertrude Lucinda Fay, 1882.

16. 79. Leonard Robert White, 1876.
80. *George White, 1879-1879.
81. Mabel Hannah White, 1880.

17. 82. *Robert Leonard White, 1866-1869.
83. Charles Dean White, 1880.

20. 84. Jessie May White, 1891.

22. 85. Hattie Marion Andrews, 1869.
86. *Minnie Bell Andrews, 1872-1873.
87. Ervin Houghton Andrews, 1873.

29. 88. Queenia Rose Tooley, 1889.
89. Minnie Lois Tooley, 1892.

35. 90. John Langworthy White, 1892.

36. 91. Albert Hopkins White, 1881.
92. Esther Evangeline White, 1883.

38. 93. Zoa May Potter, 1878.
94. Louisa Potter, 1880.
95. Jennette Potter, 1882.
96. *Alice Eveline Potter, 1887-1888.

39. 97. Franklin Chauncy Weese, 1877.
98. Walter Weese, 1880.
99. Nettie May Weese, 1884.
100. Myrtle Weese, 1890.

TENTH GENERATION.

(*Continued.*)

40.
101. Herbert Arthur Long, 1881.
102. Clara Annie Long, 1883.
103. Edith Adaline Long, 1884.
104. Emory Ambrose Long, 1886.

41.
105. Walter Elwood Hendricks, 1879.
106. Elura Hendricks, 1881.
107. Albert Jerome Hendricks, 1885.
108. Clara Hendricks, 1887.
109. Leonard Maxwell Hendricks, 1889.
110. Eva Edna Hendricks, 1891.

42. | 111. Neta Osborne Lohnes, 1890.

43. | 112. Earl Faul, 1888.

48.
113. Agnes Laura Hopper, 1885.
114. William Hopper, 1887.
115. Frederick Hopper, 1889.
116. Joseph Hopper, 1891.

49.
117. Edward Albert Getty, 1883.
118. Laura Mercy Getty, 1887.

50.
119. Richard William Getty, 1889.

ELEVENTH GENERATION.

57. | 120. Charles Edward Allen, Jr., 1889.

59. | 121. Olie Manning, 1891.

65.
122. Frances Adelaide King, 1888.
123. Clarence Roderick King, 1889.

APPENDIX II.

In the interest of accuracy of statement, as well as from a sentiment of regard for the tombs of our ancestors, I have gathered the following gravestone inscriptions. In one instance I have been enabled to correct an error, which has been perpetuated in Kellogg's "John White." Moses White died not "about 1812," but Oct. 12, 1796. Further researches of this kind will, I hope, disclose the dates of the death of Aaron Blakeslee, Ebenezer Blakeslee, and David Blakeslee. In genealogical investigations family traditions are of small value compared with the records contained in family Bibles, grave-stones, and legal documents.

(1.) From the Riverside Cemetery, Middletown, Conn.

a. "Here lyeth the body of Nathaniel White, Esq., who dyed August y⁰ 27th, 1711, aged about 82 year⁵."

b. "Here lyeth the body of Mᵉˢ Elisabeth White, the wife of Nathaniel White, Esq., who dyed in yᵉ year 1690, aged about 65 years."

(2.) From the cemetery at Middletown, Upper Houses (Cromwell).

a. "Here lyeth the body of Mᵉˢ Martha White, relict to Capt. Nathaniel White, Esq., who dyed April the 15th, 1730, aged about 86 years."

b. "Here lies the body of Enfⁿ Danil White. He was born Feb. 27, 1661, and died December yᵉ 18, 1739, in the 78th year of his age."

c. "Here lies intered the body of Mᵉˢ Susannah White, relict of Ensⁿ Daniel, who departed this life Sept. yᵉ 7th, 1754, in yᵉ 93d year of her age."

d. "Here lies intered the body of Deacⁿ Isaac White, who departed this life June 27ᵗʰ, A. D. 1769, in the 72ⁿᵈ year of his age."

e. "In memory of Mᵉˢ Sibyl White, relict of Deacⁿ Isaac White, who departed this life Nov. yᵉ 7ᵗʰ, A. D. 1782, in the 80ᵗʰ year of her age."

(3.) From the cemetery at Newport, N. H.

"In memory of Mr. Moses White, who died Oct. 12th, 1796, in the 68th year of his age.

> Friends,
> Death is a debt to nature due,
> Which I have paid, and so must you."

(4.) From the cemetery at Springfield, Erie Co., N. Y.

a. "Isaac White died Jan. 15, 1822, Æ 69."

b. "Thankful, wife of Isaac White, died June 27, 1836, Æ 76."

(5.) From the cemetery near St. Paul's church, Paris Hill, N. Y.

a. " Roderick White, born Dec. 8, 1788, in Southington, Ct., died Jan. 12, 1877.
> ' As for me and my house, we will serve the Lord.' "

b. "Lucy Blakeslee, wife of Roderick White, born Sept. 1, 1798, died Mar. 15, 1873.
> ' Her children arise up and call her blessed ' "

c. "'God is love.' Eli, son of Roderick and Lucy White, died March 17, 1840, æ. 6 years, 4 mo. & 2 days."

d. " In memory of Eli Blakeslee, who died Dec. 6th, 1826, in the 74th year of his age.
' Return unto thy rest, O my soul ; for the Lord hath dealt bountifully with thee.'—Ps. CXVI, VII."

e. "In memory of Lettice, relict of Eli Blakeslee, who died May 20th, 1830, in the 74 year of her age.
> This I desired whilst in the flesh,
>> My faith here to record,
> And tell the world in whom I trust ;
>> 'Twas in my gacious Lord.
> Then put your trust in Him alone,
>> And let your words be few,
> And look to Him for saving faith,
>> He also died for you."

INDEX.

I. Names of Descendants of Roderick White.

II. Names of persons who married Descendants of Roderick White.

www.ingramcontent.com/pod-product-compliance
Lightning Source LLC
Chambersburg PA
CBHW030855260626
47169CB00008B/2553